Victoria's Victory

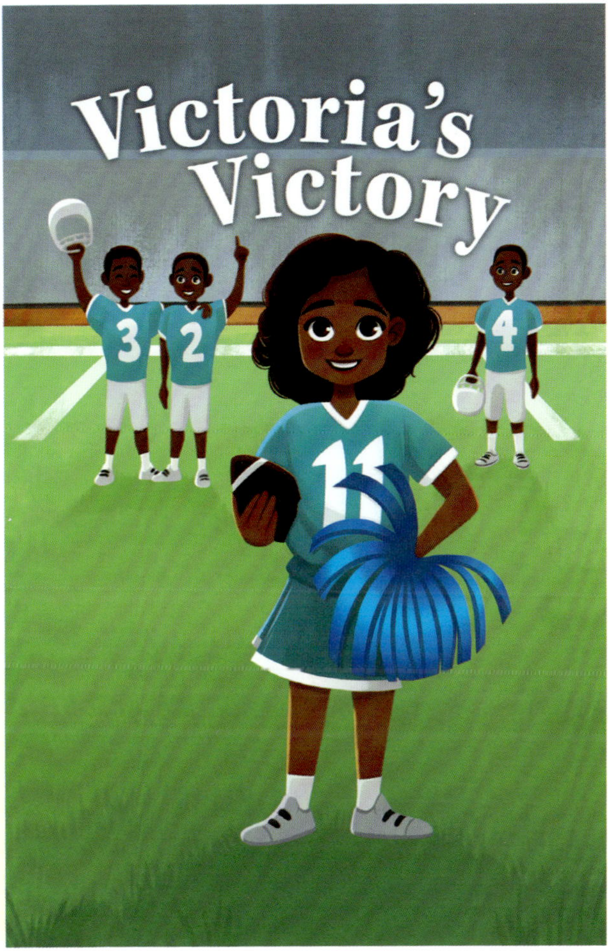

By Ivy Abby
Illustrated by Ria Maria Lee

Publishing Credits
Rachelle Cracchiolo, M.S.Ed., *Publisher*
Conni Medina, M.A.Ed., *Editor in Chief*
Nika Fabienke, Ed.D., *Content Director*
Véronique Bos, *Creative Director*
Shaun N. Bernadou, *Art Director*
Seth Rogers, *Editor*
Valerie Morales, *Associate Editor*
Kevin Pham, *Graphic Designer*

Image Credits
Illustrated by Ria Maria Lee

Library of Congress Cataloging-in-Publication Data
Names: Abby, Ivy, author. | Lee, Ria Maria, illustrator.
Title: Victoria's victory / by Ivy Abby ; illustrated by Ria Maria Lee.
Description: Huntington Beach, CA : Teacher Created Materials, [2020] | Includes book club questions. | Audience: Age 13. | Audience: Grades 4-6. | Summary: "During football season, while Victoria's rowdy and rude triplet stepbrothers get ready for the frontlines, Victoria grudgingly picks up her pom-poms and cheers for them from the sidelines. However, change is in the air this season, and Victoria's untraditional interests might inspire her entire family to change their old-fashioned ways"-- Provided by publisher.
Identifiers: LCCN 2019031481 (print) | LCCN 2019031482 (ebook) | ISBN 9781644913581 (paperback) | ISBN 9781644914489 (ebook)
Subjects: LCSH: Readers (Elementary) | Sex role--Juvenile fiction. | Cheerleading--Juvenile fiction. | Football stories.
Classification: LCC PE1119 .A225 2020 (print) | LCC PE1119 (ebook) | DDC 428.6/2--dc23
LC record available at https://lccn.loc.gov/2019031481
LC ebook record available at https://lccn.loc.gov/2019031482

5301 Oceanus Drive
Huntington Beach, CA 92649-1030
www.tcmpub.com

ISBN 978-1-6449-1358-1
© 2020 Teacher Created Materials, Inc.

Table of Contents

Chapter One: Fumbled Beginnings · · 5

Chapter Two: Having a (Foot)Ball · · · 9

Chapter Three: Backup Arrives · · · · 13

Chapter Four: Cheering
    Each Other On · · · · · · · · · · · · 19

Chapter Five: Trying Tryouts · · · · · · 25

Chapter Six: Teamwork Makes
    the Dream Work · · · · · · · · · · · · 29

About Us · 32

CHAPTER ONE

Fumbled Beginnings

Ever since I was born, there was always something different about me.

For starters, I was one of those surprise babies like on those cheesy television shows.

"Doctor, I thought I had the flu!"

"No, Vicky, you're expecting a child."

The same doctor that delivered the

news to my excited parents delivered me. I was born so early I was called a micro-preemie, and I wasn't expected to live. I did, but my mother didn't. I got a lot of things from my mother: my dimples, my curly hair, and my name. At six months old, I also got her best friend as my new mom. My dad married Rita, a single mother of triplet boys who are just a few months older than me. For six great years, we were one big happy family. Then, my dad was killed in a car accident, and Rita was back to being a single mom except now with a daughter.

Luckily, Rita is nothing like the evil stepmothers you read about in fairy tales. In many ways, Rita would treat me better than her rude, stinky boys. However, on Chore Days, she treated me like Cinderella.

"Victoria, you'll never finish sweeping if you keep daydreaming." While Blake, Jake, and Drake got to wrestle and watch sports on the weekends, Rita and I did all of the never-ending housework. "It's laundry time," Rita reminded me. "We have a lot to do this week since the boys' football season has started."

"By *we*," I asked Rita, already knowing the answer, "do you mean the boys, too?"

Rita glanced over at the triplet tornado just as Jake ripped a new hole in Drake's pants. A hole that she'd make me mend later.

"I'd sooner ask the cat," she laughed. When I didn't giggle like I usually did out of politeness, Rita stiffened up and reached for a laundry basket.

"Boys will be boys, Victoria," Rita said, offering me the basket, "and teamwork makes the dream work." How many times had I heard her say that? What about my dreams?

As I bent to pick up dirty clothes, an unwelcome breeze hit my backside. Rita forced me to mend the boys' pants but never let me wear them.

"Ladies belong in dresses," she decreed. "No *ifs*, *ands*, or *buts* about it." Mine was the only 'but' I cared about, and I didn't want it on display.

"Rita, I need a wardrobe change," I said.

Surprisingly, she agreed. "I have something you'll love!" I was speechless as she left the room, but I should have known better.

She returned carrying a blindingly pink uniform. "Our favorite color for my favorite cheerleader!"

Pink is Rita's favorite color, and she was certain it was mine, too. (It's actually brown.) Rita often said that I came home from the hospital with two accessories: a feeding tube in my nose and a pink bow on my head.

"No one knew you were a girl without that bow," she recalled as I tried on the uniform.

My cheerleading uniform was the same Pepto-Bismol™ color as that bow, and I felt nauseated wearing it.

CHAPTER TWO

Having a (Foot)Ball

The only good thing about cheerleading was football. I hated cheerleading and was terrible at it no matter how hard Rita pushed me—which was pretty hard.

"Teamwork makes the dream work, ladies!" said Rita.

Rita's favorite mantra worked on

the rest of the squad, but not on me. Football, not cheer, was the team of my dreams!

My brain couldn't remember cheer routines, but memorizing football plays was a breeze. I became a stealth expert at pigskin (that's slang for *football*), and during practice, I watched my brothers play and dreamt of joining them.

"Ignore the boys, and focus on us girls, Victoria!" Rita said.

Rita coached cheerleading like she coordinated chores: relentlessly.

I knew that if she found out I wanted to play such an unladylike sport, she would be livid. So, it's easy to understand my panic when she snooped in my room one Saturday morning shortly after I had visited the library.

"Victoria, why are your brothers' library books in your room?" I looked up from my cereal and was horrified to see Rita holding my secret stash of football books.

"Not mine. You know I don't read!"

Drake said.

The triplets are identical, but Drake is definitely the dumb one.

"Icky Vicky, why're you checking out football books? Did they run out of cookbooks?" said Jake. Jake is by far the meanest triplet.

"She's probably studying the game to improve her cheerleading," said Blake.

While Blake can be annoying (like most brothers), he's totally my best bro.

"Blake's right," I agreed. With eight expectant eyes on me, it was the best answer possible, and it satisfied Rita, who simply asked, "Are you practicing routines with Katie at the park today?"

"Going to the park now," I replied truthfully as I bolted out the door.

☙

I felt terrible walking to the park. I hate lying even more than I hate pink, but I couldn't tell Rita the whole truth, which was that I hadn't practiced with Katie in weeks.

"Hey Vic, you ready?" Junior, one of my park buddies, greeted me at the park entrance and threw me a football. A few yards away, a pick-up game had already begun.

I caught the ball and gave Junior a high-five while shouting, "Ready to play the greatest sport in the world!"

The truth was that I wasn't practicing high kicks at the park; I was kicking off football games!

CHAPTER THREE

Backup Arrives

"You played great, Victoria," Junior complimented me after our pick-up game, "and not just for a girl!"

The other players nodded in agreement, and I felt invigorated and proud, like I had won the Super Bowl.

Then, I heard three familiar rowdy voices that made me freeze—the triplets were at the park!

"I gotta go!" I threw the football to Junior and ran home. Had my brothers seen me? Probably not—the shock of seeing me holding a football and not a megaphone would have certainly been visible on their faces.

At home, I stuffed my dirty clothes in a secret backpack and hopped in the shower. As I exited the bathroom, Blake was waiting for me.

"Can't you use another bathroom?" I asked.

"I saw you playing football."

"Are you going to tell Rita?" I asked. In my heart, I already knew the answer.

"No, but I do want to help you. You're really good."

Blake's kindness was too much to believe.

"Help me do what? Mend your stinky socks?"

Blake was so used to Jake and Drake's insults that he swiftly ignored my insults.

"Technically, football teams our age are co-ed," Blake quietly informed me back in my room. "There aren't any girls right now...you could be the first!"

This sounded phenomenal but impossible, so I buried my excitement.

"Tomorrow is your last game, so I missed everything," I retorted with frustration. "Besides, Rita would flatline."

"Next season starts in six weeks, and tryouts are in a month," he said. "Don't worry about Mom."

I didn't know what to say, so I said something mean.

"Why would I want your assistance? You're terrible at football, and you don't even seem to like the sport."

Blake winced at my sharp words, clearly hurt, so I quickly changed my tone.

"I'm sorry, Blake. This is scary for me. Of course I want your help." Blake smiled, but I was still wary.

"Why do you want to help me?"

"Remember Mom's mantra?"

Blake rolled his eyes, and we said it together in our most sarcastic tone.

"Teamwork makes the dream work!"

We both fell over laughing, happier than we had been in a long time.

☙

For three weeks, Blake and I practiced every day in an isolated part of the park. First, he focused on boring basics, like a good pre-snap stance and how to point my toe while kicking.

"Blake, can't we play instead of doing this baby stuff?"

"You've got lots of natural talent," Blake said, "but even the best bread needs shaping before baking."

"That's a weird analogy—are you checking out the library's cookbooks?"

He laughed and explained, "I don't have much time to knead you into a player good enough to make the team, and I don't want you to get burnt."

During our stealth sessions, Blake was surprisingly relentless as he drilled

me on balance, agility, catching, and more until we were both sweat-soaked.

"I've never seen you play this hard in an actual game, Blake."

"That's because I don't care about the game—I care about you."

༶

I improved, and my kick went from naturally good to phenomenal!

"What can I do to thank you, Blake?" I asked.

He frowned, and I felt stupid. After all, what could he possibly need from me?

Suddenly, Blake blurted out, "Wanna teach me cheers?"

CHAPTER FOUR

Cheering Each Other On

Initially, I thought Blake just didn't want me to feel like a charity case, since cheers were all I could offer. But when he hugged me after I agreed, I knew something was up.

The triplets never hugged, they hit. Mid-hug, I was hit by an epiphany: Blake wanted to be a cheerleader! I'd been watching the boys play football, and he'd been watching me cheer!

"I was worried you'd make fun of me, Vic," Blake whispered, finally releasing me.

I found the coincidence funny, but Blake's nervousness made it clear this was no laughing matter. We both had a lot to lose—and gain—from being true to ourselves.

From then on, I taught Blake

cheers after each football practice.
He was incredible—born to cheer!
He borrowed my pom-poms, and I
borrowed his pads. It was win-win.

It was finally time for football and
cheer tryouts. Cheerleading held open
signups, so thankfully, no worries for
Blake there. What worried me was how
to tell Rita that I didn't want to cheer; I
wanted to be cheered for! But as I ate
my breakfast the morning of tryouts, my
not-so-ladylike-anymore legs spilled the
beans for me.

"Victoria, what on Earth has
happened to your pretty little legs?"

There are many reasons dresses are
awful, but number 938 is that they are
terrible at hiding bruises and scabs.
I had gotten a lot of those recently,
and Rita was horrified when she
finally noticed.

"I fell down," I said. I was too
nervous about that afternoon's tryouts
to come up with anything better.

"You're falling down on the job

to keep pretty, Miss Vicky.
Ladies should—"

"—should always have silky smooth skin with nary a blemish in sight." I interrupted. "You've only told me that one BILLION times, Rita." I regretted saying this the instant it flew out of my mouth.

"Back talk in MY house?" Rita slammed down her fork, and a piece of scrambled egg catapulted onto Drake's cheek, who was too enthralled by our fight to notice it. "What's wrong with you?"

When I tried to leave the table, Rita grabbed my arm to make me stay. That's when she noticed that my arms were worse off than my legs.

"More importantly, I want to know what's up with these atrocious cuts and bruises all over your body!"

While Blake looked horrified, Drake and Jake's grubby grins stretched ear-to-ear. Their pleasure at my pain triggered a fire inside of me, and like a long dormant volcano suddenly waking from its slumber, I exploded with my burning truth.

"Football, Rita," I spewed. "I play it, I love it, and I'm trying out for the team. TODAY!"

"Victoria, you need to call the police," Rita yelled incredulously, "because someone's stolen your mind. You can't try out for football. Girls don't play football!"

Dumb Drake interfered.

"None have before on our team, but it's legal," Drake declared.

"You are such a mom-ster, Rita!" I was almost shouting. I was livid. "I'm not just your perfect princess maid!"

As Drake and Jake laughed, I grabbed my backpack and made a beeline for the door.

"I hate cheerleading on the sidelines," I screamed as I ran outside. "I belong on the kickoff lines!"

I felt nauseated the entire walk to school. I had never even raised my voice at Rita until that moment, and I was certain I would be grounded forever. However, while part of me felt like I had fumbled, a larger part of me never felt so free. The truth was out!

CHAPTER FIVE

Trying Tryouts

"Ick Vic," Jake called across the cafeteria, "toss me your grub if you aren't eating it!"

I slid my lunch his way. I was too upset to eat anything.

"Great pass! We're gonna need all the calories we can get to survive you in tryouts!" He and Drake laughed loudly as the jerks split my sandwich.

While previously I had stressed over possibly not making the team, now all I worried about was what would happen if I *did* make the team. Would Rita kick me out of the house or ban me from playing?

By final period, I had decided to give up and not try out. But as soon as the bell rang, Blake caught me by the arm and dragged me to the field, where

I got the biggest shock of my life.

"Go, kids, go!" Rita was there, shouting her support, and she wasn't holding a cage or a leash to drag me home, but a poster that read, "Go, Jake! Go, Blake! Go, Drake! Go, Victoria!"

It was exactly what I needed to get through tryouts, which proved to be more difficult than I had expected.

Thank goodness Blake taught me drills because tryouts were an endless cycle of passing, throwing, and kicking. I looked a little silly in Blake's clothes, but I could tell Coach was impressed with me because he pushed me harder than many of the other kids. I hardly saw the triplets, but I could hear Jake and Drake taunting me almost nonstop. I say *almost* because one of my kicks was so perfect the entire field stopped talking and watched the ball soar.

By the end, I was exhausted but exhilarated and nervous. While my brothers left the field with Rita, I hung around for the 15 minutes it took to tabulate the results.

When the roster posted, Drake and Jake's names were first, followed by mine!

Blake reappeared, and I hugged him tight.

"WE MADE THE TEAM!"

"You did, Victoria. I didn't make the cutoff."

If you look up *bittersweet* in the dictionary, this moment was a textbook example. But Blake didn't look disappointed at all.

"C'mon, let's go home and tell Mom the good news," Blake said.

I froze fearfully, and Blake noticed.

"Don't worry," he reassured me, "I talked to Mom for a long time after you left. She still doesn't fully understand, but she wants us to know that she will try to support anything we do."

CHAPTER SIX

Teamwork Makes the Dream Work

"Ladies and gentlemen," Blake announced when we arrived home, "our family's first female football player!"

Even Jake and Drake cheered, and Rita wrapped me up in a big bear hug.

"Rita, I'm sorry for being rude

earlier," I apologized. "I just didn't know how to—"

Before I could finish, Rita put two freshly manicured nails on my lips to silence me. "I love *all* my children," she said, kissing my forehead, "and I want you all to live your truths."

A lot changed after that day. Jake and Drake are slightly less rude now that I'm the football team's star kicker. Rita now divides the chores equally, which I love, even though the boys turned all my white socks pink during their first load of laundry.

The last game of the season was a doozy, and winning depended on one final kick from me. I took a deep breath, focused, and BOOM! We won! I heard a giant roar from the sidelines where the cheerleaders stood.

"VIC-tory-AH! Victory for Victoria!"

Screaming the loudest of them all was my best bro Blake, in a custom cheer uniform Rita made just for him. Rita got her cheerleader after all!

About Us

The Author
Ivy Abby is the pen name of an award-winning author of multiple books for grown-ups. She is the mother of two sports-obsessed kids and encourages all young people to be whoever they wish to be, whether it is a football player, a cheerleader, or both! Growing up, Abby was a cheerleader and always wanted to play basketball, but her well-meaning mother wouldn't let her. This book is dedicated to all the people brave enough to be true to themselves.

The Illustrator
Ria Maria Lee is an illustrator who loves pretty much anything colorful, lovely, and slightly cheeky. She spent most of her childhood doodling and getting lost in books and movies. In fact, nine-year-old Lee would have been ecstatic if someone told her she would grow up to draw for a living.